Perfect Haunting

by

Steven Douglas Brown

©2020 Steven Douglas Brown

"Hell is empty and all the devils are here."

-William Shakespeare

Perfect, WA.

It started with a sound. Almost not worth mentioning. Almost. Just a *creak.* Perhaps wood tightening after a warm October day. Danny Curry only gave the sound a cursory glance. The sound came from somewhere to his right, near the perpetually ignored stationary bike and *her* end table. Two framed *(better times)* photographs, two bottles of vitamins, allergy pills, and a chunky drinking glass. Danny never touched *(shrine)* the items. Never. Staring at them, Danny quickly forgot about the seemingly random sound.

They say that time heals all wounds.

Lies.

The trauma was still there, as if her death had crudely, wantonly chopped away a piece of his soul, leaving it shredded, irreparably damaged. He would catch himself staring into space, undoubtedly a peculiar sight.

Wallowing.

Trudy would never have put up with this behavior.

Danny started to cry.

He discovered that as he got older, his emotions could not be as held at bay as easily as before; sure, he would always choke up, especially watching one of *those* dog movies. Trudy used to tease him about it, but Danny was definitely a *dog guy,* even though he had not owned one since he was thirteen years old. When asked why, Danny would always defer with a smile and shake of his head, but never answering. *No dog could ever replace Mackie.* The dog had been in the family before Danny was born and became Danny's constant companion right up to the end.

"Dang it," Danny said to himself, wiping away tears with an angry swipe of his right hand, completely forgetting the sound as memories *wrecked him,* as some of his former students would say. The thought of his former students buoyed Danny's spirits, at least for the time being. Danny had loved being a teacher.

"For all these things must come to pass, but the end is not yet."

-Matthew 24.6

Danny wrote that on the blackboard his final day teaching. Religious quotes were usually frowned upon at Perfect High School, but Danny had already tendered his resignation. *Not as if they can fire me.* Trudy opposed his quitting, but by then both knew things had gone past any personal choice.

Cancer.

The initial diagnosis nearly buckled Danny. But he had to stay strong for Trudy. But during those few moments that he was alone, Danny wept. He knew what was going to eventually happen. It was inevitable. She was gone thirteen months later. But not the way they expected. Not at all. They asked him to return to teaching afterward, but Danny was inconsolable. Devastated. That life was over. He did not believe in an afterlife, Trudy was not going to meet him on some ethereal cloud when his time came, and that was an awful truth for Danny Curry.

Alone.

Danny Curry had spent more years with Trudy at that point than the years before without her. He had intended to write a book about the experience, but ended up simply sitting in front of the computer and staring at the blank writing program, at the steady blinking of the cursor, before abandoning the idea entirely.

The road to hell is paved with good intentions.

Danny then started his daily walks. He had always loved autumn in Perfect. At least the first part. The colors. The crispness in the air. The strangely calming *crunch* underfoot. Fox Run Park. Trudy's favorite place in Perfect. Together, hand in hand, a real *Hallmark Moment,* but Trudy had coveted such romantic tropes. While he loved autumn, Danny did not like the backend, when Fall completely *fell,* paving the way for the cold embrace of winter. It was also *Fogtober,* which seemed to arrive on October 1 like clockwork. Danny loved autumn, but he did not like fog. There was something *devious* about fog to him. It seemed to *lurk.* But there was no avoiding it in October. Danny glanced around the room. The fog was out there, Danny knew without even seeing, he could *feel* it. No walk today. Not with the fog out there, waiting. Danny got up out of his chair and proceeded to turn the lights out downstairs before the ascent to the bedroom for the evening.

CLICK CLICK CLICK

Danny did not have one of those *new-fangled* voice-controlled lights and that made him feel *old.* As a matter of fact, Danny actually owned one of those voice devices, unplugged, the box opened and the small *doohickey* looked at, a freebie for something forgotten, but Danny had no desire to talk to or listen to a *machine.*

CLICK

Darkness

At that moment, Danny thought that maybe controlled lights were not such a bad idea.

The sound. Again.

Danny froze.

Dang it.

Rat.

It should have been expected with the weather getting colder, but there was still a sense of personal encroachment.

This is my house!

"Rats?"

Danny almost felt embarrassed by Wesley Hunt's question, but there was little doubt at seeing the large trap Danny had placed on the checkout counter of *Hunt's Variety Store* on Main Street. "Afraid so." The trap was bigger than Danny had anticipated. It was... *intimidating.*

Wesley Hunt rang up the sale on an old cash register, the kind where the numbers popped up to see; Wesley did have a swipe card reader for debit and credit cards, but he knew his cash paying customers liked the cash register. Old school. "Be careful setting that trap, Mr. Curry," Wesley warned, slipping the trap into a small brown paper bag. "It's definitely a finger-breaker."

Danny hesitated when Wesley handed the bag to him. "Really? Maybe I should have went with the poison bait instead."

Wesley shook his head slowly. "With this you will know where it happens, but with poison it will crawl off and you need to find it before the stink..." Wesley made a face. "Just be careful, Mr. Curry."

It was just minutes after noon and the fog still enshrouded the town. Danny could not see halfway down Main Street after stepping out of the store, tiny bag in hand. *Two blocks to home, but maybe a detour to the Pastime first.* Danny knew he was stalling. The thought of crawling under his house to place the trap was not exactly appealing to Danny. With his hands in the pockets of his jacket, head down, Danny walked the half-block to the tavern and entered. Danny found himself spending more and more time at the Pastime, sitting at the bar, watching sports, maybe turning to watch a game of 9-ball over at the two long-past-their-prime tables along the east wall of the narrow building. He never had more than a single bottle of beer the entire time he spent at the tavern, and that was more out of courtesy than anything, the bottle often not touched for nearly an hour at a time. The warm air that rolled out when Danny pulled open the heavy wood door was like a welcome embrace. No one called out his name when he walked up to the bar, the bartender barely acknowledging him, although the young man knew enough to open Danny's beer of choice and place it in front of the stool that Danny always sat on. *No more than an hour!* Danny sat down on the barstool and took out the money to pay for the bottle of beer, saying *"keep it"* to the afternoon bartender concerning the change, and then looked up at the old CRT TV hanging from what looked like a homemade mount. The sports channel. No one else was in the tavern.

"Rats?"

Danny realized that the trap could be seen, half sticking out of the paper bag in his jacket pocket. "I think so."

The bartender, a unusually young man named Mel Ryan, made a face and let out a sound from deep in his throat. "I hate rats, man." Danny expected the young man to dive deep into a personal story to back up the statement, but Mel simply let it go at that, walking away from Danny and began putting away beer glasses that had been drying on a white towel at the end of the bar.

tink tink tink

Danny rubbed his forehead with his right hand. *Stop stalling!* Then Danny realized that the access door to crawl under the house was in a closet aptly named *"the junk closet."* Danny squeezed his eyes shut, making a face. *Dang it.*

"Are you okay, Mr. Curry?"

Danny opened his eyes and saw that Mel Ryan was standing right in front of him, a look of concern on the young man's face. "I just realized that I have a lot to do before I can even get under the house." Danny slid off the table, picked up the bottle of beer and took a quick sip.

"Be careful setting that trap, Mr. Curry!" the young man warned. "I had a friend who lost a pinky because of one of those things!"

The junk closet.

It was right by the garage door and had been to go-to depository for the house's *flotsam* over the years. Danny had never considered himself a hoarder, but you simply did not know when six RCA red-white-yellow cables might come in handy or that half-a-spool of nylon string that came with the kite that he crashed on takeoff at the ocean seven years ago. Trudy had *howled* with laughter at that one, her face red, tears streaming down her face as she rolled around on the blanket spread out on the sand. *Better times.* Cardboard boxes, of all sizes and shapes, stacked easily over six feet high. *Daunting.* Then there was the smell. Mildew. Mold? Where was the moisture coming from? Maybe an investigation was in order. *Stop finding excuses!* Danny started pulling out boxes. But it was getting late and sunset was arriving earlier every day now. Were rats nocturnal? Danny hurried his removal of the boxes from the closet. Over twenty-five years of stuff. No time to look, reminisce *(get weepy),* all because of vermin. *Dang rat!* The closet was not deep, essentially just a coat closet, but Danny could not help but marvel at the sheer number of boxes he pulled out. The boxes rose around him, making Danny feel like he was a monster in a suit ready to knock down Tokyo. Then, the access door. Danny stared at it. He had things to do first. Change into crawling-under-the-house clothes. Bait and set the trap. Find a flashlight. Not stalling, necessary. Danny moved away from the closet.

    Old jeans (*tight fit*), a concert T-shirt (*Vanilla Ice?*), and then the trap. Danny put a smear of peanut butter on the metal bait *thing* and then pulled back the trap part itself. It was surprisingly hard, the tension fighting against Danny's fingers. Setting it was *scary,* the metal bar that held back the trap slipped into the bait platform. *This is so dicey!* The trap wanted to be sprung so badly, the bait platform/trigger barely keeping it from snapping shut. Even set, it seemed to *strain* hard. Danny then wondered how he would bring this thing down below without it going off. *It's definitely a finger breaker!* He picked up the trap like it was a bomb and carried it to the closet. He set the trap down on a stack of boxes and then pried open the access door in the floor of the closet. *(ugh)* The smell reached up and tore at Danny's nose as he took a small LED light from a pocket and turned it on, pointing the brilliant light down into the hole. A plastic sheet was spread out directly below the opening and Danny did not see any rat turds. *No turning back now, Danny-boy!* Danny grimaced and took a deep breath.

I'm going in!

Danny picked up the trap, placed it directly beside the opening, and then dropped in. He stomped his feet on the plastic to scare anything down below away. *Fee-fi-fo-fum.* He then ducked and took a peek. Large ducts blocked his way on three sides, leaving only one way to go; Danny quickly raised his head to get his bearings. The living room was over there, which meant he had to go around the ducts, and crawl probably twenty feet. He picked up the trap and dropped down into the hole. Moving along on his knees and one hand, the other holding the trap delicately, was not easy; the LED light was clipped to the collar of his Vanilla Ice T-shirt and the brilliant beam bobbed and swayed with every movement. Danny grimaced as he moved off the plastic and found himself on dirt. The feeling of claustrophobia was immediate, as the bottom of the house was less than an inch from Danny's head. The smell was *earthy*. Danny saw that the silver insulation for the duct system was shredded *(dang rats)* in places. He kept moving, trying to visualize where he would be if he was moving above. *Ten feet that way and the take a sharp right.* Then Danny heard something and froze.

CREAK

It was as if someone had walked directly above him; he knew exactly where that loose floorboard was that made the sound whenever he stepped on it. Danny did not move, held his breath. If someone was up there, he would hear the movement again. Then Danny heard the clock with its heavy *Westminster chimes* signaling the top of the hour. *Dang it!* The clock was so loud, whoever was up there could easy sneak off during the chiming. Then Danny dismissed the entire incident. *Who would want to break into my house? Everyone knew everyone in Perfect. Everyone.* Danny resumed his crawl.

Sharp right

Danny suddenly shivered. It was *cold!* He stopped for a moment, more because of the uncomfortable way he had to crawl under the house, the pain in his shoulders and right arm as he tried to keep the trap from *springing* before he reached his destination. There was no way he wanted to try and reset that thing down here under the house! *Just drop it right here and get out!* But Danny was the type to do things the *right* way. If he heard that rat at a certain spot, he was going to place the trap there at that certain spot. Simple as that. Danny figured he had no more than six feet to go.

What the heck?

Danny stopped again.

Fog?

Danny could not see two inches ahead of him. The LED light beam seemed to make it worse, turning the entire area ahead of him completely white. How was this possible? Danny could see the fog seem to drift in front of him, as if he was out in Fox Run Park or something. Impossible. Right?

Far enough!

Danny carefully set the trap down onto the dirt directly in front of him and was about to back away when he noticed something happening. His light was dimming. Fast. The LED was charged with a USB cable, but there was no indicator showing how much charge was left in the device.

Move!

The fog swirled.

Danny resumed backing up. He really had no room to turn around. *Slowly, but surely, Danny-boy!* How many feet back until that sharp turn?

Then the light died.

Trudy had loved Halloween.

After Labor Day, she counted down the days until October. Literally. She had a small chalkboard, initially put up in the kitchen to write out various things like grocery lists, but Trudy started her October countdown on it with her near-calligraphy-perfect script. Every morning, she would wipe away the old number *(DAYS UNTIL HALLOWEEN)* and write the next. By the second week of September, Trudy would take the large bin of Halloween/autumn decorations out of the garage and set it down smack-dab in the middle of the living room and go through it thoroughly, even though she knew exactly what was inside. The bin itself was large, orange body with a black lid. Danny had offered to bring in the bin, but Trudy refused every time.

"This is my thing," she said.

Danny understood. He considered Christmas *his thing,* so he left Trudy alone with her strange paraphernalia. Trudy was very specific concerning her Halloween decoration purchases. Nothing plastic. Or cardboard. One time, Danny had bought the classic cardboard skeleton at Hunt's store, and Trudy promptly tossed it into the kitchen garbage can, reinforcing her *no cardboard* decree. That was the last time Danny had tried to buy anything for Halloween. During a trip to Mexico, Trudy spent over three hundred dollars on a collection of Day of the Dead decorations. *Dia de los Muertos.* She loved the colorful skulls. Wood signs. Ceramics. Trudy scoured places for things that adhered to her strict requirements.

Then there was their trips to Wiseman Farm. Yes, plural. Trudy often drove by Abner Wiseman's farm in September, keeping an eye on the height of the corn and the progress of growth in the pumpkin patch. She would stop and talk with Abner, who was inhumanly patient with Trudy, if she thought the corn was not high enough or the pumpkins seemed a bit under-sized. When he caught wind of Trudy's discussions with Abner, Danny sought him out and apologized profusely.

"I appreciate her passion for autumn," Abner told Danny.

On October 1, rain or shine, Trudy and Danny went to Wiseman Farm for the first of many pumpkins would buy during the month. When he asked why she needed to go there on the first day of October, Trudy told her husband "I want the biggest and best pumpkins available."

And she did. Always.

Trudy had been on her way home after picking up another in her month-long gathering of pumpkins when the driver coming the opposite way crossed the center line. Neither had been going fast. It was foggy and the other driver was drunk and forgot to turn on his headlights. It had been fast enough, apparently.

DOA

The other driver walked away with a sore neck, but he walked away.

Danny tried not to panic. Tried. He had never experienced this kind of dark before, so total, so intimidating. Danny knew that he still had quite a distance to crawl yet. Backward. He began to move.

CREAK

That sound. Again. But Danny did not stop, determined to get out from under the house and confront whoever was up there, and then he hit his head. Hard. Enough to daze him. *Wrong way?* For a moment right after, time seemed to stand still for Danny. Stunned. He did not *see stars,* but more like a flash of light and Danny heard himself groan in pain, as if he was listening to a recording of himself from a great distance. He reached up and felt the knot and that his hair was wet. Blood? *Not good.* Danny could feel the anxiety rise, ready to tip over into a full-blown panic. He reached out blindly with his right hand. And recoiled instantly. Danny had touched something *furry.* Just brushed it with his fingertips. He jerked back so hard that he hit his head again, this time the top of his head, hitting what had to be the floor of the living room.

THUNK

And something hit the floor directly above him, as if in response.

That sound sliced through the pain and actually cleared Danny's mind.

Really?

"Hey!" he shouted. "Get the heck out of my house!" Danny reached up and pounded on the wood above his head. (*thud thud thud*) Danny fully expected a response. Nothing. He reached out again and realized that he had touched the shredded duct insulation. He knew where he was now. But the space under the house had one more trick up its sleeve.

Trudy cut her palm wide open curving a pumpkin.

"Damn," Danny had heard her say, in a tone that seemed more annoyed than anything else, and Danny figured that Trudy must have cut wrong while carving her jack o'lantern. She was very particular about her designs, needed each pumpkin to be *perfect.* With a grin, ready to tease her, Danny got up out of his chair and moved to where Trudy was sitting on the kitchen floor. Pumpkin seeds and orange, gooey pumpkin innards on a spread out newspaper. And blood. Lots of blood.

"What the...?"

Danny saw the look of anger on Trudy's face. Then he saw her right hand holding the large carving knife, her left hand clenched into a fist. Blood was seeping out from between fingers. No, *flowing.*

"Did you cut yourself?" *Such a stupid question, Daniel J. Curry! Very, very stupid!*

Trudy held up the closed fist, the blood flowing down her arm. "Looks that way, huh?"

Eighteen stitches.

SNAP

Danny froze.

The rat trap had sprung.

Already?

Then a new sound. It took Danny a moment to realize what he was hearing. The trap was being dragged across the dirt.

Toward him.

I am a rational man.

In an irrational situation.

Danny started to move again, albeit very slowly. He did not want to hit his head again.

Or let that rat know where I am.

Stop it. If it was a rat, the sound was probably a spasm and it was now surely dead. Then a thought sliced through Danny's mind, nearly surgical, flayed like the belly of a trout on a cutting board.

What if it wasn't a rat?

Danny knew the area was rife with critters. Opossum. Raccoon. Chipmunk. Squirrel. Trudy had once attempted a koi pond after seeing Bernie Bell's impressive backyard setup, and being Trudy she created a large *(and expensive)* koi pond that took over a month to finish. She went all the way to Seattle for the koi *(also expensive)* and carefully acclimated the large fish to the pond before letting them loose in their new home. The koi disappeared two days later. Baffled, Trudy bought more koi *(still expensive)* and they disappeared as well. Danny stood outside after the second time and heard the tell-tale *chittering* of a raccoon. Close. Danny did not tell Trudy about the raccoon since she gave up on the koi pond and turned it into a waterfall feature *(yes, expensive)* instead.

Danny felt the plastic and smiled in the dark. Finally. He then frowned. Danny had not replaced the access panel after him when he dropped into the hole, but he did not see the opening now. He was on the plastic sheet, for sure, and he reached up and pushed. Not there. He moved to another spot, reached up, and let out a yelp of pain. A nail? Danny could feel the blood.

Must have cut myself good.

Danny's index finger of his right hand throbbed.

Then, that sound, the dragging of the trap, closer. But another sound. Growling?

Oh, no!

Danny began hitting various spots above him.

Closer.

I'm coming to get you!

The panel. Finally.

Danny burst out of the hole, climbed out as quick as he could, and put the panel back in place. A scant second before he heard the sound of something moving on the plastic.

Close, but no cigar!

Danny walked away, inspecting his damaged digit, and did not see the access panel lift up, just an inch, and drop back into place.

Before fixing his finger, Danny checked the house thoroughly. Top to bottom, bottom to top. Closets. Behind open doors. Even under the bed. Nothing. The doors were still locked. Satisfied, Danny went to fix his finger. The *medicine cabinet* was in the kitchen.

"It's where most accidents happen," Trudy had argued when she started putting various items like band-aids, alcohol wipes, a brown bottle of hydrogen peroxide, and such into right of twin cabinets just to the left of the pantry; the other cabinets was a variation of the *junk closet,* where things like stick matches, old recipe books, and various sized batteries were kept.

After putting a band-aid on his finger, wincing against the alcohol wipe he cleaned the nasty cut with, Danny reached up and touched the large bump on his head. *That hurts!* He touched it gingerly, could feel the crust of dried blood in his hair. There was no way he could manage a band-aid there, so he took out a new alcohol wipe and dabbed at the knot. Danny let out a shriek. *Definitely hurts!*

Trudy had always been the accident prone one. It became a running joke between them over the years. Danny knew that she would be giving him a hard time right now.

(if)

Danny stood in the kitchen and stared at the alcohol wipe, at the blood. *Accident prone.* He walked out of the kitchen and went upstairs for the night. It seemed like the walk up the stairs got harder. No more taking steps two at a time anymore. When he was young, at his parents' house, Danny used to *jump* down the stairs, hitting the landing with a loud *THUD* after leaping down over four steps. Just the *thought* of doing that made Danny's knees hurt now. *So long ago.*

"Stop *jumping,* Danny!" his mother would shout each and every time he came down the stairs.

"Listen to your mother, Danny-boy!" his father would say afterward, although it sounded more like a bored addendum.

Danny entered the bedroom and shut the door behind him. Locked it. *Habit. That's all.* He grabbed a remote control off the bed and turned on the large TV mounted on the wall. *Background noise.* He used to grade student test papers with the TV on, learned to completely ignore what was on the screen. It was early. Danny did not like being downstairs after dark.

Especially tonight?

Danny changed into sweat pants and a clean T-shirt and then stretched out on the bed. Right side. His side. The king size bed seemed so enormous now.

Maybe I should *get a dog.*

Abner Wiseman said one of his dogs had puppies recently and offered Danny pick of the litter. Abner's dogs had loved Trudy. Wagging tails. Happy howls. Trudy had a nickname for every dog. *Floppy. Silly. Lolli. Boomer. Precious. Goofball.* Abner told Danny that it got to the point where the dogs only responded to Trudy's nicknames.

Maybe I'll go to Abner's tomorrow. Maybe.

Danny glanced at the pill bottle on his nightstand. Sleeping pills. Dr. Cook wrote him essentially an open-end prescription for them… after. He had offered Danny tranquilizers, but Danny passed.

Not tonight.

Danny actually looked at the TV screen. A beer commercial. He wished a football game was on, but it was the wrong night. Danny loved watching football. Danny and Trudy had met at a football game.

The Perfect High School football team were not exactly living up to the town's name that year. Winless. Danny had a lot of friends on the team and felt obligated to go to the games. By mid-season, the stands were not exactly standing room only. Even the parents of players found excuses to not show up. At the time, Danny was working part-time at Nate Crenshaw's video store just off Main Street and got up after checking his watch, seeing that his shift was going to start within the hour. "Hey!" he heard a voice call out when he started moving down the metal bleachers, the *CLANK* each footstep made very loud, all but announcing that he was leaving. "Where do you think you're going?" Danny looked around and saw two girls huddled together several feet away. It was Trudy and Sally Barton, twin sisters.

"I have to go to work," Danny called out. He knew Trudy and Sally, at least by sight, having seen them in the halls of Perfect High. He was not sire which of the two had called out.

"Fine," Trudy said. "But I better see you here next week!"

Danny had to smile and offered the girls a wave as he left.

At the next home game, Danny found Trudy Barton alone in the stands. Her sister, Sally, had broken up with Fred Sawyer, the captain of the football team, and did not want to go to the game whatsoever, but Trudy was a fan of the game. Trudy and Danny started talking football. Before halftime, Danny realized that Trudy was practically a walking encyclopedia on football and was amazed. Before the game was over, Danny knew that he was in love with Trudy Barton. Trudy, on the other hand, was not as equally smitten with Danny Curry. But Danny was tenacious. *I have all the time in the world.*

Danny could already feel an ache settle in from his time under the house and he grimaced as he stretched. *Getting old sucks.* For a moment, a very *quick* moment, Danny considered going out to his work shop and start a new furniture project. Once upon a time, Danny Curry enjoyed making furniture pieces. End tables, coffee tables, the occasional chair. But he had not touched his equipment since the funeral.

funeral: an end of something's existence

Danny inhaled deeply and let it out slowly.

These moments seized him unexpectedly.

melancholia

No one blamed him, to the point of avoidance. There was an *awkwardness,* that inability to interact with *the widower.* Danny knew that he may as well had T-shirts printed up. The stigma.

Danny felt himself in that strange place between being awake and being sound asleep. He was aware that the TV was still on, but his mind was a kaleidoscope of nonsensical dream images.

knock knock knock

Danny's eyelids fluttered and he sat up, a confused look on his face. Was the knocking in his dreams? Danny shook his head, to clear away the final figment. He turned off the TV and listened. The sound did not return.

To die, to sleep - to sleep, perchance to dream - ay, there's the rub, for in this sleep of death what dreams may come…

Hamlet… dude.

Danny rolled over onto his left side, staring at that *enormous* empty space beside him.

Trudy used to snore. Not all the time. Cute, short snorts.

"I don't snore!" She had been quite indignant when Danny mentioned it to her one morning when Trudy complained that her throat was dry, so Danny quickly changed the subject, and recorded her snoring on his phone that night.

Danny picked up his phone off the end table, brought up the clip, and placed the phone on the other side of the bed. He closed his eyes, listening to the soft snoring, and fell asleep.

Danny could not find his phone the next morning. Figuring he must have knocked it off the bed in his sleep, Danny checked the floor, under the bed, but did not find it, leaving him more perplexed than angry. He quickly put it out of his mind for the time being, because he had something else to deal with that morning.

The trap.

Danny went downstairs and paused at the closet door.

Do it later!

Danny had a puppy to pick out.

Having to use his land line phone *(like a caveman!)*, Danny called Abner Wiseman and asked if the offer to pick a puppy was still open. Abner sounded delighted and confirmed that the offer was still indeed open. Danny told Abner that he would drive over immediately and hung up the phone.

The noise.

Danny shook his head. He grabbed his car keys off the hook near the kitchen door and walked to the garage door, pausing again at the closet. It was early, he could check the trap later. Danny opened the door to the garage.

I'll need to buy puppy food!

Danny found himself surprisingly excited as he got into his car.

Maybe a few toys, a bed.

He opened the garage door with a remote attached to the sun visor and backed the car out.

Danny took the long way to Wiseman Farm. He still could not bring himself to drive on *that* road, pass the spot where the accident happened.

He did not know the man who killed his wife, the man was not a local, was just passing through the area. The man had not fled the scene. He stayed, told those

(I'm a god-fearing man!)

who would listen that he tried to save Trudy, was holding her hand when she died. The man was not technically drunk, was below the limit, but had enough for him to forget to turn on his headlights on a foggy evening, crossed the center line due to not being familiar with the road.

(god-fearing!)

There were moments when Danny was *jealous* of that man. His face was the last face that Trudy ever saw. *His! A stranger!* When they had gotten the cancer diagnosis, Danny had readied himself for that moment, the possibility that he would be there, holding her hand as she passed. But, in the end, it was not his face that Trudy saw when she died.

Danny started crying.

He slammed his hands on the steering wheel.

STOP IT!

He had to pull over and wait until he composed himself.

The puppies were running around inside a barn when Danny arrived. There was no small talk, that awkward silence settled in as Abner Wiseman took Danny to pick the puppy to take home. Danny knew that Abner felt tremendous guilt, others told Danny that Abner said if Trudy had never gone to Abner's farm she would never had been on that foggy road with that other *bastard driver.* Danny never felt that Abner was at fault, not in the slightest, but the California transplant kept the guilt, tight, like a cloak of shame he would never shed. People were already out in the pumpkin patch when Abner and Danny neared the barn; Danny realized that he had not picked up a pumpkin yet and felt more than a little embarrassed. Here he was, asking for a puppy, and had not even bothered to get a pumpkin from Abner! Danny could hear little *yips* from inside the barn, sharp, chirp-like barks, and he smiled in spite of himself. The noises sounded so *alive*. "Which one had the puppies?" Danny asked, breaking the silence.

"Floppy."

Danny then saw Abner quickly turn away, Abner realizing that he had used Trudy's nickname for the dog; Danny could see Abner's lips were tight and knew the man was trying hard to keep a sob at bay. It had been an expression Danny was quite used to sporting almost on a daily basis. Danny patted Abner on a shoulder, and Abner nodded. A sound from Abner, deep in his throat, and a quick wipe at his eyes. They entered the barn.

The puppies were glorious. They immediately crowded around Danny and Abner. Fluffy. All paws and lolling tongues. Danny smiled and bent over to pet each of the seven puppies. "Oh, they're all so cute!"

Abner frowned. "One of them is missing." He looked around the barn. "There she is!" Abner pointed upward. A white puppy was up on a hay loft, looking down at them. "How did you get up there?"

Danny walked up to the hay loft, and the puppy jumped, Danny catching it deftly. "Oh, definitely this one!"

"Are you sure, Mr. Curry? This one seems... *crazy!*"

"I'm sure."

Danny ended up calling the puppy *Snowball*. He did not see any separation anxiety at all as he carried the puppy to the car.

"You have everything you need?" Abner asked as Danny climbed into the car, placing Snowball on the passenger seat; the dog looked straight ahead, tail wagging.

"I'm going to Hunt's right now, called ahead to make sure he had everything."

Abner nodded his head and smiled at the puppy. "Don't be a stranger, Danny."

Not wanting to leave Snowball in the car when he got to the store, Danny tucked her in down the front of his jacket, head and front paws sticking out.

"OH. MY. GOD." That was Betty North at seeing Snowball. "That's the cutest thing ever!" Betty had both hands on her cheeks. "What's her name?"

"Snowball. How do you know she was a she?"

"I can tell."

Wesley Hunt rolled his eyes. "Leave the man alone, Betty."

"You hush your head, Wesley!"

Wesley, behind the cash register, double-checked the dog supplies he had placed on the counter in front of him.

"Oh no!" Betty exclaimed. "You are *not* feeding this precious thing *that* garbage!" Betty picked up the puppy food with two fingers and flung the bag up a nearby aisle.

"I fed my three dogs that food when they were puppies!" Wesley argued.

Betty walked off and returned with a different brand of puppy food, and then Wesley and Betty got into an argument over the two puppy food brands.

"How about we try both?" Danny quickly handed Wesley his debit card.

Wesley and Betty were still arguing when Danny and Snowball left the store.

With Snowball still tucked securely in his jacket, Danny got out of the car, the garage door still closing behind him. It made an uneasy *screeching* sound that always bothered Danny. "We're home, Snowball." Danny gathered the recently purchased dog stuff and went inside. Danny immediately filled one of the two small bowls with water and filled the other with puppy food; he looked around, trying to figure out the best spot to place the two bowls. He set them down in the kitchen next to the center island, where he usually had his breakfast every morning. He took Snowball out from his jacket and set the puppy down on the floor. "I don't know the last time Abner fed you," he said to the small dog. "I should have asked him." Danny made a face at himself for the mental slip. He watched as the dog seemed to regard her surroundings for a moment and then took off in its goofily adorable amble. "Where are you going?" Danny smiled as he watched the dog explore the area. Danny followed Snowball into the living room, watched as the puppy sniffed the carpet for a few seconds and then promptly flopped onto its belly and went to sleep.

I should do something to thank Abner.

It was at that moment that Danny decided to get back to making furniture.

Danny had taught shop class at Perfect High and supplemented the household income by creating various pieces of furniture in his workshop. He had not made anything since the funeral. Danny stood, staring at the puppy sleep, lost in thought. *What would someone like Abner like?* Something functional. Something sturdy. But Abner came from LA, worked in the movie business. *A little flash, too?* Danny needed to find a pen and notebook to do some sketches. He walked out of the room.

Snowball raised her head with an inquisitive chirp.

When Danny returned to the living room, he was surprised to see Snowball near the *(still ignored)* stationary bike, pawing at the floor. He watched as the dog tilted her head this way and then that way before continuing to paw at the floor.

The trap.

Danny had completely forgotten about it. He knew that he needed to go back under the house and retrieve the trap before it started to *stink.*

Later.

Danny swept up the dog and sat down, the puppy on his lap. Snowball continued to look toward the area where it had been pawing, but quickly fell asleep again. Danny sketched furniture ideas with one hand and gently scratched behind Snowball's left ear with the other hand.

This is very relaxing.

Danny let his eyes close.

Trudy never visited Danny in his dreams and that was a constant source of frustration. Danny anticipated sleep in hopes of dreams of her and woke disappointed every time.

All that we see or seem is but a dream within a dream.

Poe.

Danny clung to the hope that ole Edgar Allan was spot on. *Hasn't it been long enough?* At least there had been no nightmares. Danny's dreams were always nonsensical. Fragments. Completely random and did not relate to reality whatsoever, from what Danny could remember when he woke. Since they had nothing to do with Trudy, he dismissed the dreams without bothering to seriously recall them.

Danny did not feel Snowball slide off his lap, tumbling to the carpet awkwardly. But he did hear when the puppy started to bark, if you could call it a bark, as it sounded more like an adorable *squeak.* Danny jumped up out of his chair and followed the sound, finding Snowball standing in front of the closet door, continuing that squeaky bark. "You hear something?" Danny asked, sweeping the puppy up with his right hand and bringing it to his chest, protectively. Snowball moved to look toward the closet door and let out a little growl. *Maybe she smells it, maybe it's rotting already.* Danny knew he could not put it off much longer, but he did not look forward to crawling under the house again. Not at all.

Danny spent the rest of the day doing *puppy stuff.* Making sure Snowball ate enough, drank enough. Laying down training pads to hopefully avoid expected accidents, but Snowball seemed extraordinarily adept at utilizing the pads. "Good girl!" Danny would say, like a proud parent. Then night fell. Fast. "Time to go upstairs," he announced to Snowball. Danny picked up Snowball, the dog bed, and the one toy the puppy seemed to enjoy the most. He was about to leave the room when he let out a grunt of surprise. His phone. Right there on the island. He swept it up, put it in a pocket, and continued upstairs. Danny had planned to place the dog bed on the floor next to his side of the bed. First he led Snowball explore. The puppy sniffed. moved, sniffed, and then spent a few seconds chasing her tail. Danny turned on the TV and got on the bed, sitting up against the backboard, watching Snowball continue to explore. He would start work on his gift to Abner in the morning, and that meant a trip to get the right wood for the project.

Should I take Snowball with me?

Of course he would, she might hurt herself alone!

Danny heard a tiny whine and looked down to see Snowball, both front paws up on the side of the bed. "No," he said. "Your bed is right there." Danny was worried that Snowball would fall off the bed and possibly break something. But then Snowball let out one of those barks that sounded more like a squeak and started to jumped up, trying to reach the top of the bed, only succeeding in falling back onto the floor. "Fine," Danny said, reaching down and picking up the puppy, putting her on the bed. Snowball immediately moved to Trudy's side of the bed, turned in circles three times, and curled up into a tight ball, burying her snout under her hind leg. The puppy was asleep in seconds. "Wow…" Danny said to himself. *Maybe I can make some kind of guard rail for that side of the bed.* But Danny had no problems, since Snowball continued to sleep soundly, not moving from her spot on the bed.

Danny did not sleep well that night. He kept waking and checking on Snowball, but the puppy never moved. At 6 AM exactly, Snowball let out a huge yawn, got up, stretched, and then sat down and looked at Danny, tail wagging.

"Good morning."

Snowball chirped/barked.

Danny did not think the dog actually answered him, but could not help but smile fondly at Snowball. "We have a full day ahead of us, young lady. Are you ready?"

Again, the chirp/bark.

Danny carried the dog downstairs and made coffee while Snowball hit the training pad, receiving another enthusiastic "Good girl!" from Danny. While Danny sat at the kitchen table, drinking his coffee, Snowball explored. Danny was surprised at how comfortable he was having the dog move around freely. He walked into the living room, took out his computer tablet, and checked the news for anything interesting, while Snowball continued her solitary exploration. The town's newspaper, *The Perfect Times,* had quite an impressive online presence and Danny did not feel as bad that the print edition pretty much went extinct, although he did miss the feel of newsprint in hand on chilly autumn mornings, the damp smell as the seemingly ever-present October fog almost permeated every page. After (Danny referred to everything post-funeral as *after),* Dave Casey offered Danny a weekly column in the then-new online edition of *The Perfect Times.* "I'm not a reporter," Danny told Dave.

"You don't have to be," Dave replied. "Just write whatever comes to mind."

Danny graciously declined.

But now, his right index finger poised over the computer tablet to swipe to the next page, Danny wondered if maybe he should have taken the offer. *Not a reporter, definitely not a writer!* He shrugged to himself and finished his coffee. First thing's first. "Snowball, time to go!" The dog ran/hopped quickly to Danny, who smiled as he picked her up. "Good girl!"

Burt Arrow was surprised when he got a call from Danny Curry, asking if Burt had a certain wood available to purchase. Yes, he did have the wood. Hell, he would have specialty ordered it for Danny if he didn't even if it cost Burt money in the end, because it was nice that Danny was back to making furniture.

"My, my!" Burt exclaimed when he went out to meet Danny. "Who do we have here?"

Danny had Snowball tucked in his jacket again; it seemed natural, for both, already. "This is Snowball."

"Perfect name! Abner?"

"Yes."

"Outstanding. But you won't be packing Snowball around like this much longer."

"Why not?"

"Look at the size of those paws! I'm guessing Snowball here will easily be close to a hundred pounds when she grows up."

"Really?" Danny looked down at the puppy. "We might have to change your name to *Avalanche* by then."

"I have the wood you want right in here." Burt waved an arm and both men walked across the small parking lot into a building where Burt stored his available wood supply. The wood came in various shapes, sizes, some cut, some natural, virtually every type of wood a person could think of, placed in separate sections.

Danny inhaled deeply. He loved the smell of the different wood at Burt's place. As they walked to where the particular wood Danny asked for was set aside, Danny took note of different piece of natural, uncut wood for potential future projects, that old enthusiasm rising in him. "How much for that piece?"

Burt smiled. "It's nice to have you back, Danny."

Am I back?

Danny felt strangely affected by what Burt had said to him. He did not *feel* back. Danny put Snowball down and then unloaded the wood, placing the pieces *(way more than I should have bought!)* in the middle of his workshop. Snowball sniffed the wood and then sneezed. Danny regarded the wood pieces, trying to *see* the furniture in them before starting the long process. He was going to make Abner a coffee table, a very ornate coffee table. Danny glanced at his sketches, now stapled to a nearby wall. *Too ambitious?* Danny knew there was only one way to find out. He picked up a carpenter pencil and stood over the large piece of wood he placed on his work bench. He started marking the piece of wood. He did not see Snowball slowly turn toward the workshop door. The fur on the dog's back rose and she began to growl. Danny did not notice, concentrating on his new project, until the little dog started to bark its less-than-threatening squeak/bark. Danny slowly turned toward Snowball. The workshop was a pre-fabricated, stand-alone shed that was tucked in a corner of the backyard. Danny had an electrician run a proper line in for power and had the whole shed sound-proofed so not to disturb the neighbors. That alone made Danny surprised by Snowball's bark; he usually could not hear a thing from outside.

tap tap tap

Something was hitting the outside of the small building.

"What the heck is that?"

The sound was light and Danny might not even have noticed if not for the dog's reaction.

tap tap tap

Danny picked up a rubber mallet off his workbench. "Come here, Snowball." The dog offered a growl and then moved to stand in front of Danny, who reached down and picked her up. He held the dog in the crook of his arm and moved to the door. "Maybe it's that raccoon," he said to Snowball. "One way to find out." Danny opened the door, mallet raised.

Nothing.

Danny leaned out through the open doorway, looking left and right, Snowball doing the same. Neither Danny nor Snowball saw anything. Satisfied, Danny closed the door and set the dog down, returning to his wood sketching. Snowball sat down next to Danny, still looking toward the door. Two hours later, Danny let out a frustrated grunt. *It's not working.* He threw down the carpenter pencil on the worktable. "Let's call it a day," he told the dog. "No use trying to force it."

Anticipating being picked up, Snowball got up on her hind legs, front paws on Danny's left leg. Danny reached down and picked her up, moving to the door.

BAM BAM BAM

The pounding was loud. Heavy.

Startled, Danny actually jumped backward.

"That's no raccoon!"

Snowball started barking and Danny rubbed her head, trying to calm the dog down, while trying to regain his composure. *Someone's out there!*

"Who's there?" he shouted. No response. Danny picked up the mallet again, moving to the door. "Too bad you're not already big," he muttered to Snowball, the dog squirming in his arm, trying to jump down, wanting to attack. "Calm down," Danny whispered to the dog. Danny felt uneasy. Unusually so. He did not want to go look.

Man up!

Easier said than done.

Danny absently scratched the top of Snowball's head. Listening. Where was it now?

It?

Danny saw Snowball's ears *twitch*. The dog's head slowly turned, from right to left, as if she was tracking something.

It's stalking us.

It. Again.

How many steps to the back door of the house? He had walked the route so many times in the past that the grass had been worn away, like a game trail in the wilderness.

25? No. More like 30.

Cougar? Bear?

Perfect was surrounded by the forest, the town butted right up against the Cascade Mountains. Danny had heard others in town talk about run-ins with various wildlife coming into backyards, but never experienced such an encounter himself. Other than the raccoon that ate Trudy's koi. Maybe it was just a deer. How embarrassing would it be, cowering in his shed because of a cute little lost fawn?

"What do you think, Snowball? Should we just go for it?"

Snowball yipped.

Danny nodded. "Good enough for me."

When he opened the door to his workshop, Danny was surprised that darkness had fallen already, hard and deep. That meant the house was dark, too, as it was still light out when Danny and Snowball entered the large shed.

As a kid, Danny had been scared of the dark, as most kids were wont to, wrapping himself in his bedding at night, leaving only the smallest opening to breathe. He thought he never knew the reason for his fear, it was just *there,* waiting for him every night. If hard pressed, a young Danny would say it was because of the *Boogerman* (not *Bogeyman,* that would come with adulthood), but young Danny knew it was actually something else, something to do with the area. Bad things seemed to happen in Perfect's neighboring towns. Evergreen. Amber. Danny's friends would spread the rumors about those towns on the playgrounds or during sleep-overs, passing it along like a verbal virus.

The Dead Land.

Young Danny knew it came from an Indian (not *Indigenous People,* that would come with adulthood) phrase he could not pronounce. But it was an *ugly* sounding phrase. Billy Lee, a friend from grade school who moved between the fifth and sixth grade, once claimed that the towns of Amber and Evergreen were actually built on *ancient Indian burial grounds,* and that was why bad things happened. But young Danny thought Billy's theory was farfetched, if not downright *stupid.* In all of his years up to that point (all nine of them), young Danny had never seen a single, honest-to-goodness real life Indian outside of a John Wayne movie, so why would they have a burial ground someplace like Evergreen or Amber?

"You ever been to Evergreen?" Billy shot back at young Danny's dismissive call-out at recess one late winter afternoon. "I have!" Billy then gave a breathless, obviously exaggerated version of the Evergreen he saw, not bothering to say he saw the town when his father got lost one day and had to stop and ask for directions at the *Evergreen Cafe* on Main Street, staying in the town for a whole five minutes altogether before they hit the road again. As far as Billy Lee was concerned, Evergreen was where the monsters lived.

With Snowball held in his right arm, Danny looked out through the open doorway of the shed. No deer. No bear. No cougar. Danny wondered what had hit the side of the shed, but did not want to investigate. Not in the dark. Danny was no longer afraid of the dark, he did not sleep in a protective cocoon; actually, Danny often went without any covers as he slept, but he still did not let his leg drape over the side of the bed. No use pushing the odds. It turned out to be fifty steps to the house. *Nice calculating, Curry!* Danny and Snowball entered the house. Food, water, training pad, and then upstairs.

Billy Lee might have been way off on his *Indian burial ground* theory, but he was definitely right about there being something *wrong* with the area.

Evergreen. Amber.

Perfect?

Horror would come to town, but that was another story.

The smell.

Danny began to catch whiffs of it the next morning. Even Snowball noticed. The dog stood staring at the closet door while Danny drank his morning coffee. "I know what I have to do," he said to the dog. But he needed to prepare himself first. Rubber gloves were brought out from under the kitchen sink; Danny had plenty of them, bought to use when he stained furniture he built, Trudy always buying them whenever she found them on sale. Danny then tied a bandanna over his nose and mouth against the stink. Danny opened the closet door and looked back at Snowball. "I'm going in," he intoned seriously. "You stay here." With the LED light clipped to the collar of his T-shirt (this time the shirt had *LAS VEGAS* blasted across the front in vibrant colors), Danny pulled open the access panel and peered down into the hole. He had hoped that the trap would be *right there,* that he would just have to reach down and pluck it out, but no such luck. Danny dropped to his stomach and lowered his head into the hole, looking around. The sprung trap was nowhere in sight.

Shoot!

Danny was about to drop into the hole when he heard knocking, three sharp raps.

Not again!

But Danny saw that Snowball was wagging her tail and looking toward the back door. Danny replaced the access panel and looked toward the door.. "Who is it, Snowball?"

"Mr. Danny...?" a muffled voice was heard.

It was Teddy Jones. Next door neighbor. Teddy was *slow.* Danny believed that the current term was *intellectually disabled.* But Danny had heard worse things. Kids could be cruel. But so could some adults, even unknowingly.

"You still helping that retarded kid?" That had been Danny's father last Thanksgiving.

"Dad, we don't call them *that* anymore!"

Albert Curry looked puzzled. "That's what we always called them."

"It's not politically correct."

"What the hell does *politics* got to do with it?" Albert Curry looked even more puzzled.

Danny opened the back door.

"You going candy hunting, Mr. Danny?"

"Huh?" Then Danny realized that Teddy meant *trick or treat* because Danny still had on the gloves and bandanna. "Oh. No, I was about to go under the house."

"Why?"

Danny wondered if he should tell Teddy about the trap, not knowing if Teddy understood the concept of pests. "Something smells bad under the house and I was going to go get it."

Teddy turned around and took a step before he flinched and turned around to face Danny again. "Do you want me to go, Mr. Danny?"

"No, Teddy. I can do it later. Come on in. Besides, I have something new to show you."

"Your new doggie?" Teddy flinched again. "I'm sorry. Mr. Abner told me yesterday when I went to his farm."

"Snowball," Danny called out. "Come here, girl."

When Teddy saw the puppy, his hands flew to his face and he let out a shriek, which promptly scared off the dog. "Oh, no! I'm so sorry, Mr. Danny!"

"She's a puppy, Teddy. They scare easily."

"I can be real quiet, Mr. Danny." Teddy put a finger to his lips and went *Shhhhhhhhh!*

Danny smiled and waved Teddy inside. "I'll go get her and introduce you two."

Teddy began to wring his hands, excited, his left foot tapping quickly. Suddenly, he stopped. A frown appeared on his face and he started to shake his head rapidly, so forcefully that it looked painful.

"No, no, no, no, no, no…!" His voice rising, until he was shouting, causing Danny to run into the room, holding Snowball.

"What's wrong, Teddy?"

"I want to go home!"

"What happened?"

Teddy backed up until he crashed into the door. "I saw it!"

Danny looked around. "What?"

"That… *thing.*" Teddy's features screwed up in concentration as he tried to verbalize what he had seen, but the connections were not aligning and Danny could see the growing frustration on Teddy's face. "What's always with you in the light!" Teddy then turned and pulled open the door, hesitating a moment before fleeing. "But it wasn't with anyone! It was by itself!" He ran off.

Danny slowly closed the door. He looked down at Snowball in the crook of his right arm. "You understand that?" he asked the dog. Danny had to decipher Teddy's often incoherent, scattershot way of talking in the past, but this was different.

That... thing.

"I'll talk to him about it some other time," Danny said, glancing toward the closet door. "How about we go work on Abner's present instead?" he said to Snowball, opening the back door again and moving out into the yard, toward the work shed.

What's always with you in the light.

Danny opened the door to the shed and entered, placing Snowball on the floor as he shut the door behind them, pausing, looking down at his feet as he mulled over Teddy's puzzling words.

It was by itself!

Danny had tried initially to teach Teddy, but it was a slow, frustrating process. Teddy simply could not process anything beyond kindergarten level. Teddy was as sweet as the day was long, perhaps too sweet. Teddy had the penchant to trust everyone. Teddy's mother worried about that tendency and asked Danny if he could help teach her son that not everyone could be trusted. That had been seven years ago, and Danny knew that Teddy still remained blissfully ignorant of the evils that men do.

"Where's Mrs. Danny?"

Danny had not been in a good place at that moment and Teddy's innocent question *broke* Danny. Broke him hard. He fled Perfect. Danny did not like thinking about that week after he left Perfect. Las Vegas. Red eye flight. Danny knew it had been a half-assed suicide attempt disguised as non-stop drinking and gambling. He returned to Perfect in even worse shape, shaky, mentally fragile, and sixteen thousand dollars richer due to an amazing run at a craps table. After he returned, he noted that Teddy never mentioned *Mrs. Danny* ever again. Sadly, Danny later realized that Teddy has simply *forgotten* Trudy completely.

"Let's get to work," Danny said out loud and picked up a wood chisel.

This was the most unkindest cut of all…

Danny forcefully buried the chisel into the piece of wood.

Hey, STUPID!

For some unfathomable reason, a half-way house for *mentally challenged (*that had been the go-to term at the time) people was opened less than half-a-block from Perfect High. Teenage Danny knew that nothing good would come from the close proximity of his school and *Century House*. He was not wrong.

You know why they call it Century House, dontcha? Because it has a hundred idiots living there!

Actually, it was not a house, but a smallish, horseshoe-shaped apartment building. While the majority of the student body ignored the place, there had been a small group of teens who saw the residents of Century House as easy prey. Every school had those kind of kids. Bad seeds. Bully was too easy a description, as far as Teenage Danny was concerned. Those kids were *sociopaths.* But for another unfathomable reason, that group of teens *liked* Danny Curry. He never sought out their friendship, but that group always seemed to gravitate to him. Maybe it was his long, shoulder-length hair. Maybe his *school uniform* of concert T-shirt and jeans, a different band every day. Teenage Danny lost count how many times someone would stop him in the hall between classes and ask if he had any weed to sell; it got to the point where he gave his pat answer of "No, man, I'm all out." *That* group was mostly of a nebulous count, faces came and went, the only constant was the sheer *cruelty* toward anyone not one of them. Once, a new *member* of the group made the mistake of shoving Teenage Danny against the lockers after Danny's usual denial of having any weed to sell. Big mistake.

"You touched my bro?" a voice boomed behind the soon-to-be unfortunate shover. The voice belonged to Bruce Albert. While the group had no real leader, Bruce was the most-feared. The seventeen year old looked like a thirty-five year old biker, complete with motorcycle leathers and a full beard. The hall cleared fast.

"I'm sorry, Bruce!" the newbie stammered. "I didn't know!"

Bruce walked up to Danny, leaned toward him. "You okay, bro?"

"I'm good, Bruce. It was just a misunderstanding."

Bruce then grabbed the new guy by the back of the neck and led him out of the building.

What scared Teenage Danny the most was that no one ever saw that guy again.

The Century House caught on fire one night. Luckily, no one was hurt, but the residents had to be moved elsewhere after; some heard they went to Amber, while others heard they were taken to *Klondike Peak,* a mental institution up in the mountains. No one was ever charged for the obvious case of arson, but Teenage Danny knew better. *They* liked him and talked freely around him.

I was hoping for retard flambé *myself!*

Teenage Danny kept his mouth shut.

Guilt.

Is that why you help Teddy?

Danny slammed the chisel down on the work bench. He had cut himself. "Dang it," he mumbled to himself, looking at the cut on his left hand. Not long, but deep. Blood pulsed out, oozing down into his palm. Stitches? Then the shed *shuddered.* Besides fog, October was also the start of the windy season in Perfect. Winds would funnel out through the mountain passes with a ferocity that seemed to get worse every year. 50-60 MPH wind was now commonplace in October and November. Snowball lifted her head and let out a concerned bark.

"It's just the wind," Danny said. Another strong gust. Rattling. "But we better go inside. I don't feel like ending up over the rainbow today." Danny picked up Snowball and stood at the door, waiting for the gust to subside. He opened the door and moved out of the shed.

Perfect was surrounded by ancient evergreens and they *howled* in the wind. The sky was angry. Seeing things flying through the air, Danny covered Snowball protectively as he rushed to the back door. He then saw a bright flash in the sky to his left and figured that a power line had gone down.

No power now. Just great.

Danny could tell the power was out because Trudy's waterfall stopped, the pump dead in the water, pun definitely intended. He entered the house, hand immediately swiping at the light switch just inside, causing Danny to chuckle at himself. *You knew the power was out, Edison!*

How long until sunset?

It was already semi-dark inside the house due to the outside gloom. Danny put the dog down. He needed to break out the flashlights and battery-powered lanterns. No candles. Danny had a thing against candles. *They're dangerous.* Snowball ran off, disappearing in the growing darkness inside the house. "Don't go far," Danny called out. He walked into the kitchen and pulled open the drawer where he kept *things,* stuff needed, but not all the time. Spare bolts. Wire. A pencil. He was looking for a set of battery-powered push lights, the kind where you pushed on the dome part on top and it lit up red, blue, green, or white, depending on how many times you pushed the dome. He found one. *Better than nothing.* He pushed the dome part. Nothing. Needed new batteries. He unscrewed the bottom. Three AAA batteries. He pulled the drawer open farther, pushed aside a bunch of household *jetsam,* suddenly realizing that he was getting blood all over the inside of the drawer. He needed to tend to his cut. Back to the medicine cabinet. *I'm just the walking wounded lately.* The bump on his head was still tender. Concussion? *Don't be so dramatic!* He wiped the cut with an alcohol pad, hissing in pain, and then wrapped the finger with a bandaid.

"Snowball?" Danny realized that he had not seen or heard the dog in a minute or so and did not want to lose her in the encroaching darkness. "Come here, girl." Silence. *This isn't good.* Danny cocked his head, hoping to hear the dog, but only heard the wind outside. Before, Danny had always grinned ruefully at people he saw who treated their dogs like their children, but now he could relate because Danny could feel an anxiety grow at the absence of Snowball. He walked out of the kitchen, whistling, quick, short. "Snowball!" Darkness was almost ready to fall on the house completely and Danny had to turn on his little LED light. He let out a gasp. The closet door was ajar. He rushed up to it and pulled the door open all the way, inhaling so sharply that it hurt his chest. The access panel in the floor was pushed aside, easily big enough for a dog to fall in if too curious. Danny dropped to his knees and leaned over the hole in the floor. "SNOWBALL!" Only cold air and the growing stench answered Danny. *This isn't good at all!* Danny clenched his jaws and dropped into the hole. *If anything happened to her...* He gagged. The stench was awful. He pulled the collar of his T-shirt over his nose, but the thin material did little to block the smell. *What the heck died down here? An elephant?* Danny's eyes were actually watering.

"Snowball...?"

Danny wished that he had brought a plastic bag along with him, to put the sprung trap in when he found it; if it stunk this bad now, he could not even imagine how bad it was going to be when he came across the trap and its unfortunate victim. He followed the duct and was about to take that sharp right turn around it when Danny saw something that caused him to let out a shriek of sheer and absolute terror.

Something peeked from around the duct at him.

It was black, the kind of black you would think belonged in the deepest reaches of outer space. Then it pulled back behind the duct and disappeared.

Danny screamed again, but was froze, unable to move.

Stress chemicals. Prefrontal cortex shutdown.

Danny had learned about traumatic experiences while still teaching, when school shootings across the country caused the school district to send out an internal memo about post-trauma situations and how to deal with them.

Then Danny heard Snowball bark, above him, muffled, and the fear-induced paralysis broke. He scrambled backward and sprang up out of the hole, gasping, face covered with sweat. Snowball was right there and jumped into Danny's arms before he pulled himself up out of the hole.

Minutes later, Danny was pounding nails into the access door. "Screw the smell!" He drove in no less than a dozen nails. Overkill? Danny did not care. When he closed the closet door, Danny entertained the idea of nailing it shut as well, but decided not to go that far.

Yet.

Snowball sat watching Danny the whole time.

Danny looked down at the dog after he finished. "I think that's good enough." He picked up Snowball. "Where were you, missy?" Danny could hear the wind storm still roaring outside. "Who knows how long the power will be out," he said in low tones, walking into the living room. He could already feel a chill in the air. "Better make a fire, I guess." Danny put the dog down and moved to the fireplace. One of the reasons why they bought the house was because of the fireplace. Trudy loved it, but they ended up lighting it maybe only three times, and two of those times was due to the same reason why Danny set about getting it ready to be lit at the moment. *Old ashes, old memories.* Danny twisted a newspaper (not *The Perfect*

Times, but one from Big City) and tossed it onto the andiron, topping it with some kindling and then placing a large piece of wood on that from a rack of wood beside the fireplace. A long stick match, struck against the brick mantle, ignited the paper quickly and soon there was the satisfying sound of crackling wood, a glow and warmth coming from the hearth. Danny sat down in the large leather easy chair in front of the fireplace, Snowball on his lap.

What was it?

As he sat staring into the flames, Danny tried to recall what he had seen under the house. It happened so fast, literally just a couple of seconds, and the whole thing was already disappearing in a memory haze. *Dissociative amnesia?* Danny had dismissed the whole thing when he received the school district memo as *"fancy talk,"* but Trudy had chided him at the time.

"It's the times we live in, Daniel!" She only used *Daniel* when she wanted to make a point, pretty much a declaration that *You better pay attention, mister!* She was worried about the spat of school shootings, worried because the kind of students that took Danny's shop class were not exactly the *academic type,* more prone to the behavior that led to such terrible incidents.

"In Perfect? Come on!"

"That's probably what they thought in Columbine."

Danny knew not to argue with his wife when she got that passionate about a subject.

It looked like a shadow.

Danny then let out a little gasp.

What's always with you in the light.

Teddy was trying to describe seeing a shadow.

But Teddy saw it in the kitchen.

It had been up here?

Danny felt himself shudder, an uncontrollable reaction.

Pareidolia

Just seeing things.

Danny knew he was just trying to convince himself.

It was a dark and storm night… and the monsters were ready to fight.

Danny took out his phone and opened a search engine, typing in *Shadow Figures.* He was astonished at how much was out there on the subject. Danny spent the next hour reading various stories about encounters with the so-called *Shadow People.* Then his phone died.

"Oh, great!" Danny shook his head at himself. "Way to go, Danny!" What if there was an emergency?

Next… on When Shadow People ATTACK!

Danny let himself sink deeper into the leather easy chair. It was almost time to put more wood on the fire. But not right now. Danny had to let things sink in a bit.

Was this a haunting? Or something else?

Danny wanted to dismiss it as sheer *happenstance.* But he knew that sometimes *2+2 = weird.* Maybe it was Billy Lee's Ancient Indian Burial Ground trope come home to roost.

I shall not commit the fashionable stupidity of regarding everything I cannot explain as a fraud.

Jung.

Danny recalled what he read on his phone. There were as many different theories about them as were stories. Some said ghosts. Demons. Inter-dimensional beings. Even aliens.

Pick one.

Danny did not believe in ghosts or demons. Inter-dimensional beings? *Well...* As far as aliens, the possibility was there, but one knocking around under Danny's house stretched the credibility of that one very thin.

It's because the power is out. Get ahold of yourself, Danny-boy!

Trudy, on the other hand, would be *loving* this stuff. That was a given. Trudy had always been disappointed that her birthday came on November 3.

"Four days! I missed having the *perfect* birthday by four lousy days!"

Trudy watched horror movies all October, watched all the paranormal shows on TV, and went all out with the front yard decorations. When she saw Christmas stuff being brought out in stores before the end of October, Trudy would rant about it for *hours* when they got home, and Danny could only listen silently, knowing better than to interject or interrupt.

WWTD?

Danny knew Trudy would definitely try to contact whatever it was, with more enthusiasm than Danny could possibly muster. Truth was, Danny no way wanted to contact what he saw under the house. *No, sir!* Contact? He did not want to *see* it ever again.

Maybe it was the fire, maybe it was the earlier stress, but Danny fell asleep in the easy chair.

Dawn.

Snowball was still on Danny's lap. The fire in the fireplace was nothing but cold ashes. Was the power still out? The dog jumped to the floor as Danny got up out of the chair and groaned loudly. *Too old to be sleeping in a chair like this!* He winced in pain. *Stiff neck.* Danny moved to the kitchen and saw flashing digital numbers on both the stove and the microwave, telling him that the power was indeed back on that morning.

Coffee. Puppy food. Fresh water. After both Danny and Snowball finished, Danny decided to go outside to check for any wind damage. Snowball bypassed the training pad and waited by the back door for Danny.

"You actually want to *go out*?" Danny reached down and petted Snowball. "What a good girl!" He opened the door and the dog rushed outside. Danny followed and looked around while the puppy moved to the lawn and *did her business.* Nothing seemed to be damaged, although the back yard was now strewn with what looked like cedar boughs blown in from somewhere around the area. Trudy's waterfall was quite loud in the post-storm silence. Danny often found Trudy sitting near the cascading water after he finished his last class for the day. Sometimes she had her eyes closed, just listening, other times she would be reading. Always a book about the paranormal. *Was that normal? Her seeming obsession about the paranormal?* She had been getting into learning about the history of Perfect's *Headington House.* It was not hard, especially since the release of *that* movie. Danny wondered if this was how it was to live in Amityville; it was as if after that particular movie, Hollywood seemed to want to make a movie about any small town haunted house. Personally, Danny thought the *Simpson House* over in Evergreen was more terrifying than the Headington place, but the whole town of Evergreen seemed to be under some kind of non-disclosure mandate. Trudy had gone around and talked to anyone who was around when the *Headington Incident* happened.

"Why is your wife snooping around *Headington business?*" someone at the local grocery store had asked Danny one time, practically cornered him over by the breakfast cereal aisle. A lot of the local *old timers* did not like people bringing up the past, especially after the obviously sensationalized version of *The Perfect Demon House* that played at the Perfect Movie Theater, bringing in too many *outsiders,* asking about the house and having to be chased off the property by the Perfect police. When he got home, Danny told Trudy what had happened, but she just laughed it off.

The wheel jerked out of my hand.

That had been Troy Walsh during the trial. It had been ignored, an excuse, but the words came back to Danny now. He wanted to hate *(I'm a god-fearing man)* Troy Walsh, but the man seemed completely devastated.

Get in line.

The hate would come later.

"It was that fog," Walsh said. "I couldn't see past the hood of my car."

The fog.

Danny would find her siting here by her waterfall, in the fog, a strange smile on her face. Danny did not like that tableau, one of the very few that he put away in that bottom mental file cabinet drawer. To Danny, she had always been too *accepting* of fog, and in the end, it was the fog that had killed her, as much as Troy Walsh's fateful crossing of the center line.

Snowball started barking.

The dog was over by Danny's workshop. The bark sounded angry, not your typical *there-goes-a-squirrel* bark.

"What's wrong, Snowball?"

He expected the dog to be by the shed, but Danny found Snowball along the side of the house. Danny rarely used swear words, thought they were a crutch, but occasionally one would slip out.

"Oh, shit…"

Something had dug a hole, a *big* hole, along the base of the house. How long had it been there? Danny did not see the displaced dirt anywhere near the hole and then he realized that Snowball was too close to the hole for comfort. He quickly swept up the dog into his right arm, her usual spot, and backed away from the hole.

That's how it got under the house!

But the *it* was definitely bigger than a rat.

Danny knew he had to fill in that hole.

"Hi, Mr. Danny!"

Danny was startled. Snowball let out a frightened *yip* as Danny jumped and spun around, finding Teddy standing directly behind him. He tried to smile at Teddy, but knew it probably looked more like a pained grimace. "You scared me, Teddy…"

"Oh, no! I'm sorry, Mr. Danny!" Teddy then saw the hole in the ground and his mouth actually dropped open. "Wow! Look at that!"

"You ever see a hole that big around here, Teddy?"

"No," Teddy said, moving closer and then dropping to his hands and knees, peering down into the hole itself. "It goes right under your house, Mr. Danny!"

"I need to fill it right away."

"I can help!" Teddy jumped back onto his feet, raising his left arm high into the air, like a kid in class with the right answer to a teacher's question.

"I think to be on the safe side I better fill it in with gravel and rock."

"We can use my daddy's truck and go to the Pit."

Danny had borrowed the truck in the past, was on good terms with Teddy's folks, so off to the Pit they went ten minutes later.

The Pit.

It was just outside of town, hidden in the evergreen trees that surrounded Perfect, a failed gravel supply business. The pit itself was slowly being filled with water, but no one would ever dare dive in; the water was stagnant, stunk like rot, and was probably filled with so much bacteria that if you ever stuck a toe in the *water* it would possibly rot off immediately. But locals helped themselves to the rock and gravel that had been piled high just to the west of the large pit.

"How much do you need?" Teddy was ready to go to work, eager, bouncing up and down on the bench seat beside Danny in the cab of the truck. Two shovels and two large plastic buckets rattled in the bed of the truck.

"Better get extra, just in case."

"It's an awfully big hole, Mr. Danny."

"Yes, it is." Danny parked the truck beside the large gravel hill. "Thanks for the help, Teddy."

"I like helping, Mr. Danny."

They got out of the truck, grabbed the shovels and buckets, and dug into the gravel. They worked in silence, the only sound was the shovels digging into the gravel hill, the gravel being dumped into the buckets, and then emptying the buckets into the back of the truck. After ten buckets of gravel, Danny told Teddy it was time to find large rock.

"How big?" Teddy asked.

"Bigger the better. I want to place them all around the house to hopefully keep it from digging again." Teddy nodded and ran toward the rock pile. By the time Danny caught up with him, Teddy was already trying to lift an enormous rock. "Not that big, Teddy!" Danny was worried that Teddy would lift himself straight into a hernia.

"Oh. I'm sorry, Mr. Danny."

"Don't be sorry, Teddy. But lifting something that large and heavy could hurt your insides."

"It could?"

"Yes."

"Hurting your insides doesn't sound good."

"It isn't." Danny knew from experience. He had a hernia, not serious enough to need surgery, but something that reminded him every time he tried to lift something too heavy with a dull ache just to the left of his navel.

Teddy lifted a basketball sized rock with ease. "How about this big?"

"Perfect, Teddy. Let's make a pile here and then I'll drive the truck over so we can load them."

"Deal!" Teddy started grabbing large rocks and piling them.

After they loaded the rock, Danny stretched and let out a groan.

"Are you okay, Mr. Danny?" Teddy asked, sounding concerned.

"I'm fine. Just adjusting the kinks."

"Huh?"

Danny smiled and threw a rock into the large, water-filled pit. "Let's go." They climbed into the truck. Neither saw a rock come flying out of the pit, hitting the tailgate of the truck.

"What was that?" Teddy asked.

"I must be going too fast. Just one of the rocks bouncing around in the back."

Back home. Refilling the buckets with the gravel and taking it to the back yard was tiring, even for the unflappable Teddy. It took longer to unload than it took to load the truck at the Pit. Finished, Danny wiped the sweat from his forehead.

"Thank you, Teddy!"

"It's always good to help you, Mr. Danny!"

"How about I take you to the movies this weekend?"

Teddy's eyes lit up and he started bouncing from one foot to the other in excitement. "Really? The movies? The *real* movies?"

"If it's okay with you parents."

"I'll ask now!" Teddy ran off.

Danny smiled, but the smile disappeared. "I guess I'm filling this hole by myself." He picked up the shovel and started tossing gravel into the large hole. He threw in a few of the larger rocks and then gravel again, layering it between the two until the hole was filled. Danny then placed three large rocks on top. His old hernia screamed in protest. *Pay for this tomorrow!*

"I can go!" Teddy shouted, running into the back yard. He then stopped, seeing that Danny was finishing up with the hole. "Oh, no! I should have stayed and helped you with that! Oh, no!"

"It's all right, Teddy. Saturday afternoon?"

"What about Saturday afternoon?"

"The movies? I'll pick you up."

"Oh, yeah! The movies! Yay!" Teddy started dancing in tight circles.

"I'm going in to clean up. You should do the same."

"Yes. Clean up. Yes. See you later, Mr. Danny!"

Teddy ran off again.

Danny realized that he should have given Teddy the truck keys. *I'll go drop them off later.* He walked into the house.

The Perfect Movie Theater. It being October, Brad Warren had scheduled a month-long selection of horror movies, a different sub-genre every week. There were zombies movies, the Slashers, Universal Monster movie week, and *The Classics.* At least classics according to Brad Warren, and since he was the owner of the movie theater, no one could say much. Danny did not want to take Teddy to see something overtly frightening, but luckily that week the theater was showing a collection of Universal monster movies. Saturday was a triple feature of *Creature from the Black Lagoon, Revenge of the Creature,* and *The Creature Walks Among Us.* Although he did not like the idea of leaving Snowball alone for the length of a triple-feature, the dog seemed content, curled up on the foot of Danny's bed. Danny had already decided that he would stop at the pet store on the way home and pick up a special treat for Snowball after the movies.

Teddy was almost beside himself with excitement as he and Danny walked to the movie theater; practically everything was within walking distance in Perfect. There was a noticeable autumnal chill in the air that late afternoon and Danny shivered inside his jacket. *Time to haul the winter gear out of the closet already?* But Danny just blamed it on his age, as Teddy did not seem affected by the chill whatsoever, practically dancing a jig beside Danny the entire way to Main Street.

"Is this scary, Mr. Danny? I like scary, but not *scary!*"

"It's not too scary, Teddy."

"Good. Because I like scary, but not *scary!*" he repeated, undoubtedly without realizing it, a trait Teddy had whenever he got too excited.

Danny looked up and down the street. Jack o'lanterns were already lit in front of the stores. Danny knew that in a couple of weeks, Bruce Garden would transform Main Street from Halloween to Christmas overnight, driving his sputtering pickup to the head of the street and work his way down Main, hanging decorations, all before sunrise the first of November. Some in town openly complained that things should not be put up until at least after Thanksgiving, but they were in the minority, and Bruce himself stated that since winter often came in hard and fast before mid-November, he probably could not decorate Main Street due to the frigid winter temperatures once December rolled around. *Take it or leave it.* They took it.

There was actually a line when they arrived at the theater, mostly older people who wanted to relive some memories while watching the old Universal movies. Teddy looked up at the glowing theater marquee and tried to say the title of the movie, but could not get past the word *creature*. It came out sounding like *kree-a-too-ree.* The line moved quickly and soon they were inside the theater, and promptly got in another line, for the snack bar.

"Popcorn?" Teddy asked, sounding excited all over again.

"What's a monster movie without popcorn?"

"Oh, boy!" Teddy started his hopping jig again.

"Calm down, Teddy."

Sandy Ford was behind the snack bar counter and smiled brightly as Teddy and Danny moved to the front of the line. "Hi, Teddy! Hi, Mr. Curry!" Sandy had been at Perfect High when Danny was still teaching and they saw each other in the halls occasionally.

"We'll take a large popcorn and two sodas, please," Danny ordered.

Still smiling brightly, Sandy nodded and turned around to fill the order.

"Soda?" Teddy asked in hushed tones to Danny. "I've never had a soda before, Mr. Danny." He sounded like someone had just offered him his first beer instead of soda pop.

"You're old enough, Teddy."

Teddy's eyes got wide as Sandy placed the two sodas on the glass counter, followed by an enormous tub of popcorn. "Wow..." Teddy whispered.

"Oh!" Sandy said as Danny picked up the popcorn and sodas. "Don't forget your 3-D glasses!" She reached under the counter and brought out a pair of cardboard 3-D glasses and handed them to Danny, who smiled as he accepted them.

First soda AND 3-D?

Danny knew that Teddy was definitely in for a new experience.

They entered the theater auditorium and picked their seats. Halfway down, dead center. A few people called out greetings to Danny, who waved back, and then he and Teddy settled into their seats, Danny handing Teddy his soda and 3-D glasses. Teddy held both like they were strange artifacts dropped out of the sky, or something. Danny placed the tub of popcorn on the armrest between them. As he munched on popcorn, Danny looked over and realized that Teddy was still looking at the soda in one hand and the 3-D glasses in the other like he had no idea what to do with either of them. Then the lights went down in the auditorium and Danny took the glasses from Teddy's hand and placed them on his face.

"It looks *weird,* Mr. Danny!"

"It will get better once the movie starts."

Danny spent more time watching Teddy's reaction to the movie than the movie itself. First of all, he had to keep himself from laughing at seeing Teddy wearing the goofy 3-D glasses. Teddy's expression went from excitement to wonder as the 3-D movie started. He ducked, he reached out to the screen, he cringed. Danny ate popcorn, one kernel at a time, and thoroughly enjoyed the time with Teddy.

"Thank you, thank you, thank you, Mr. Danny!" Teddy exclaimed as they left the movie theater.

"I'm happy to do it, Teddy."

"Are you going home now?"

"No, I have to stop at the pet shop to get something for Snowball."

"Can I come along?"

"Of course."

They walked up Main Street. The fog was creeping in already, moving around the trees beyond town, looking like they were just waiting for the right moment to invade the town proper.

Fair is foul and foul is fair, hover through fog and filthy air.

Danny knew any given situation had an accompanying Shakespeare quote right on the tip of his tongue. Trudy used to say that he should have been an english teacher instead of a shop teacher, given his devouring of so many tomes, everything from Billy S. to Carl Jung to Tolstoy to Twain.

"An english teacher is nothing but a frustrated writer," Danny told Trudy. "I'm not a writer."

The pet store had quite the unique odor when Danny opened the door and he and Teddy entered. Teddy immediately leaped sideways as a large white cockatoo let out a *squawk* just inside the door. It raised its spiked yellow crest and let out another *squawk* for the hell of it as Teddy stumbled away from the large bird.

"I don't like that!" Teddy said of the bird on its large wood perch.

"Why not?"

"It's got a *black tongue,* Mr. Danny!" Teddy shuddered.

"Hi, Fred!" Danny called out to the owner, Fred May, who was restocking something on shelves to their left, taking the items from a cardboard box on the floor and lining them up.

"Howdy-do, Danny! What can I do you for?"

"I'm want to pick up something for my dog."

Fred stopped restocking at this news. "You have a dog now?"

"Got it from Abner."

"I see! That new litter." Fred smiled. "Puppy toy!"

"Definitely."

Fred waved him over to the dog section and the two started looking at various items as Teddy moved toward the back of the store. "Can I go look at the fish?" Teddy asked no one in particular.

"You go right ahead, Teddy!" Fred called out. "Just don't let the piranha get you!"

"Oh, I won't!" Teddy moved into a separate room where illuminated fish tanks lined the walls, two high, easily sixty tanks carrying a variety of aquatic denizens. Fresh water, salt water. The walls of the room were painted black to enhance the tank room experience. After the mind-bending (for Teddy, at least) experience of watching *Creature from the Black Lagoon* in 3-D, this trip to the tank room seemed... *boring.* Teddy usually found it an exciting visit, but the fish were just... *floating.* He pressed his face against one of the tanks, trying to replicate the 3-D, but it just was not the same. Teddy left the room a bit disappointed. He found Danny at the checkout counter, paying for Snowball's new toy.

"Ready to go, Teddy?"

"Yes. Thank you, Mr. May." Teddy followed Danny out of the store.

Danny took Teddy home first and then cut across his back yard and entered his house, quickly checking the now-filled-in hole before entering.

"Snowball, I got you something!" he called out, shrugging off his coat.

Nothing. No scrambling of paws on the wooden floor upstairs, no whining at the top of the stairs because Snowball still had not successfully made her first descent herself yet. Danny frowned. Worried. He had left the upstairs light on in the bedroom for the puppy, but it was now pitch dark downstairs. Paper bag in hand, Danny moved to the stairs and looked up before ascending.

Something looked back down at him.

It was the shadow.

Danny let out a startled shout and the dark figure pulled back out of the sight. Danny ran up the stairs. "You better not have touched my dog!" he shouted, angry. "SNOWBALL!" Danny hit the top landing and looked around, seeing nothing, but there was no doubt in his mind that he had seen the black shadow that time. It was solid, but Danny could see no features whatsoever. It was simply a black shape. Danny ran into the bedroom and found Snowball sitting on the bed, wagging her tail, looking obviously happy to see him. Danny ran up to the bed and grabbed the dog, holding her tight against his chest and he turned and slammed the bedroom door shut, locking it. Danny then made a face. He looked down at Snowball. "I know, you have to go out." He took a deep breath and then unlocked the door, opening it quickly and sticking his head out, looking around before dashing to the stairs and running down, Snowball in his right arm. Danny ran to the back door and opened it.

Outside, the fog was back. Danny set the dog down on the lawn and stood just beyond the door, looking back inside the house. "Seems less spooky out here in the dark than it does in there," he said to Snowball. Danny purposely left the back door open. He did not want another *surprise* when he went back inside.

How do you set a trap for something like that?

Danny stared at his house, arms crossed, rubbing his chin with a forefinger.

Trudy probably would have known.

Then a thought formed, more of a memory, pulled up from the depths of the bottom drawer of that mental file cabinet. Trudy's books. She had many books on the paranormal. Too many. But Danny could not get rid of them *after*. They were up in the attic. It was not really an attic, but there was an access panel, like for under the house, but in the laundry room. The area above was unfinished, not a true attic, but Danny had put some plywood up there to rest on the studs. He placed a lot of her stuff up there, knowing it would be safe and dry.

Danny glanced upward for a moment. The laundry room was next to the bedroom. He looked down at Snowball. "I have to get the ladder."

First, food and fresh water. First things first. Danny stood watching the small dog eat, lap some water, eat the rest, and finish up with more water. "Good girl!" He knew that he was stalling. He did not think that *thing* would be up there, that would be *way* too cliche, but seeing all of Trudy's stuff would be hard.

Trudy broke up with him on graduation night. No one knew, people always saying that they had been the *perfect couple,* but there was always something behind perfection that had to be kept hidden to maintain the facade. She had told him that it just wasn't working for her. Right in the middle of his graduation party, up in his bedroom. Danny had been devastated *(wouldn't be the last time)* by her declaration. He got angry.

"Then get out!" he shouted, his voice drowned out by the music from down below. They did not see each other again for three months. *She's on vacation,* he had lied to his parents about why Trudy had not been seen all summer. For the first time in his life *(wouldn't be the last time),* Danny had considered suicide. *Teenage angst.* Danny found the idea laughable now, all these years later. They reunited by sheer accident. Literally bumped into each other on Main Street. The rest, as they say, was history.

Danny pushed up on the panel above his head, shaking his head as particles of *something* came down into his face, momentarily blinding him as some of it got into his eyes. *Dang it!* He closed his eyes, but did not rub them. It burned. He could feel tears squeeze out. He slowly opened his eyes and climbed up, sticking his head up into the attic, looking around. It was warm up there. *Wasted heat.* The boxes. Fifteen. Each one marked with Danny's scrawl. CLOTHES. MAKEUP. SHOES. PURSES. BATHROOM. PHOTOGRAPHS. He had to push aside a few of the boxes to find the one he was searching for, but did find it behind the box marked VACATION. He had to actually crawl halfway into the space to grab the box marked BOOKS. He half-expected that dark *thing* to appear, pop up like a demented Halloween prop, but nothing happened. He pulled the box across the plywood and brought it down into the laundry room. It was heavy. Danny left the ladder in place in the laundry room so he could return the box later.

Danny took the box into the bedroom and set it down on the floor, Snowball inspecting it with several sniffs. "All good?" Danny asked. The dog sat down and watched. The box was heavily taped. "I kind of went overboard," Danny said, taking out a pocket knife and slicing the tape. The knife was old. He got it from his maternal grandfather when he was ten years old. *Never know when you might need to cut something. Or someone.* Grandpa Simon had been like that, saying off the wall stuff just to get a reaction. He had been Danny's favorite. Danny opened the box and let out a low whistle. The box was full of books. Hardbacks. Paperbacks. The smell of old books wafted up into Danny's face. He took all of the books out and placed them around him in a circle. He did not know where to start. "What do you think?" Danny asked Snowball. The dog wagged her tail but said nothing. Danny picked up the book directly in front of him and checked the Table of Contents for any hint of something worth reading. Nope. Back in the box. All of the books were *non-fiction* (Danny nearly let out a snort of laughter) and seemed to cover essentially the same stories over and over, except one book. Adam Burke was the author. The title of the book was *Making Horror.* Danny started to read, opened the book to a random page. *Evergreen?* Danny quickly checked the book flap for information about the author. Adam Burke wrote those horrible *Bump in the Night* books that were made into the equally horrible movies. Adam Burke lived in Echo Ridge, no more than thirty miles from Perfect. Then Danny found something in the book that surprised him. It was autographed. Personally. To Trudy.

Trudy... I hope you find what you're looking for! ARB~

Danny put the rest of the books back into the box, taped the box shut again, and returned the box to its spot in the attic space. He then took the Adam Burke book and stretched out on the bed, starting to read from the beginning. *What was Trudy looking for?*

"Hello?"

"Hello, Mr. Burke. My name is Dan Curry."

"I'm sorry, but this is a private-"

"I'm Trudy Curry's husband."

A long pause.

"What can I do for you, Mr. Curry?"

"What do you know about *shadow people?*"

"Oh, shit..."

Adam Burke looked *haunted* to Danny. That was the only way he could describe the author when they met. Danny had never been to Echo Ridge and found it to be a very nice place, even if it made Perfect look like Big City in comparison. They met at a cafe that had outdoor seating out back which offered a downright breathtaking view of Mt. Rainier. Danny ordered a club sandwich, while Adam ordered triple espresso.

"That looks... potent."

Adam smiled. "I have a lot of writing to do later."

"Oh, am I keeping you? I'm sorry!"

"No, I write at night." Adam then frowned as he watched Danny wrap his sandwich in a paper napkin and put it in a pocket. "Diet?"

"Oh! I'm saving it for my dog. I know it's probably bad for her, but I'm only giving her a little and save the rest for when I'm working."

"Working? Teaching again?"

Danny hid his surprise. How did he know? "No, I make furniture sometimes and I'm making a piece for a friend who gave me my dog. It's a thank you for Snowball."

Adam smiled again. "Snowball," he parroted back to Danny. "I like that name." The writer sipped his espresso. No change of expression, as if he sipped water. "What's happening, Mr. Curry?"

Danny told Adam everything, it all coming out and leaving Danny nearly breathless afterward. Adam listened, did not interrupt. After Danny finished, Adam downed the rest of his espresso in one gulp and stood. "Let's go," he said.

Danny blinked. "Where?"

"Your place. I need to see this thing!"

"How did you know Trudy?"

Adam smiled. "She came to a book signing in Seattle for *Making Horror* and told me that she hated the *Bump in the Night* series."

"Sounds like Trudy."

"As a writer, you can only appreciate such bluntness."

Both men were standing in Danny's driveway.

We're stalling.

"We better go inside," Danny finally said. "I don't like leaving my dog in there by herself."

They entered the house.

Adam stood in the living room, his eyes darting back and forth, while Danny went to get Snowball. The writer did not move. Almost as if he did not want to give away his location. To Adam, it was like different lyrics to the same old song. He spoke at lectures, saw the eye rolls, heard the *clucking*, and rolled with the verbal punches during the Q&A after. They knew recent revelations about famous cases and interrogated Adam mercilessly.

They claim not to believe, but they still listened. Just in case.

Adam was not surprised that Dan Curry sought him out, because Curry had not been the first.

"This is Snowball," Danny announced when he returned.

Adam could not help but smile. "What a cutie!"

"Say hello to Mr. Burke, Snowball."

The dog *yipped*.

"Did you teach her that?" Adam was impressed.

"No, she's just that smart."

"She might be able to help us."

"How?"

"Pets can sense things, even see things we can't see."

"I don't want to do anything that can get her hurt." Danny actually turned away slightly from Adam, bringing the dog in even closer, protectively wrapping his arms around Snowball.

"We won't let anything happen to her. She will just be our... *barometer,* in a way."

"What do we do?"

"Just watch her." Adam could see that Dan did not want to put the dog down. "She'll be fine," he reassured.

Danny set Snowball down on the floor. The dog sat and looked up at the two men. Snowball looked at Adam and then Danny, yawned, and then curled up into a ball on the floor and fell asleep.

"She *is* just a puppy," Danny said.

"Where did you see... *it*?"

"At the bottom of the stairs and under the house."

"Any poltergeist-like activity associated with those sightings?"

"I'm sorry, Trudy was into that stuff, not me." All Danny knew about poltergeist was that it was the name of some movie that Trudy made him watch one time, although he found it all very silly and Danny actually started to doze off before the end.

"Have you seen things move? Doors opening or closing on their own?"

"No, but I did hear footsteps, and something pounded against my shed outside."

Adam still did not move. *I'm out of my depth here.* He had never experienced the *shadow people* phenomena, but it intrigued him greatly. *Another book?* Adam almost felt guilty. Almost.

"What was that inscription you wrote in Trudy's book?" Danny asked. "*I hope you find what you're looking for.*"

Adam tried to recall his short conversation with Trudy. The problem was that the *afflicted* flocked to him. Book signings, lectures, conventions. Adam tried to offer as much as he could, given his limited knowledge. It was almost terrifying to Adam, having these frightened, *damaged* people asking him what to do to stop the torment.

"She said something was happening in Perfect and she wanted to figure out what."

What was happening in Perfect?

"She didn't say?"

"No. Compared to others I talk to, she was very cryptic."

"That doesn't sound like Trudy. She was always very *accessible.* She didn't hide anything."

"I remember that she seemed very... determined."

"Now that sounds more like Trudy. If she put her mind to something, she followed through to the end." Danny then frowned to himself.

To the end.

The wheel just jerked out of my hand.

The connections were made in Danny's mind and he put a pained expression on his face. "It killed my wife."

Adam could not, did not want to believe what Danny Curry had just said, but it did not feel like wild desperate straw-clutching from a shattered widower. To Adam, it seemed *possible*. "We need to be careful, Dan. Very careful."

"What's happening here, Mr. Burke?"

"Call me Adam, please. I think we will be spending a lot of time together to figure this out."

"What do you want to do first?"

"Check out the Headington house."

"I was afraid you were going to say that."

The Headington House.

It looks my parents' old place.

Adam had seen the movie. T*rue events.* He now realized that Hollywood had done some exterior *embellishments* to make it look spookier than it actually looked in real life. It looked exactly the same as all of the houses up and down the street.

"Did Trudy ever come here?"

"I don't think so, but she could have when I was still teaching."

"Think we can go inside?"

Why?

"I'm sure we can find a way." Danny motioned for Adam to follow.

They found a way inside, via a broken basement window. It was a tight squeeze *(too much pizza)* for Danny, but he managed.

"What are we looking for in here?"

"Demons?"

"You're kidding, right?"

"I hope so." Adam took out his phone and turned on the flashlight app. "But I don't need a lame horror movie to tell me something weird happened here."

"People died. That's not weird, that's tragic."

"I know all about people dying, Dan. Too well."

"They made movies from your *Bump in the Night* books, but not your last one. Why?"

"Because I dared call it non-fiction. If I wasn't so high profile due to my earlier books, I would have been *disappeared* for telling what actually happened."

"That sounds a little *New World Order-ish* to me."

"My publisher dumped me, my agent dumped me, and I had to put out *Making Horror* myself. You might call it being paranoid, but I call it reality."

"Look, I'm just an old ex-shop teacher. Show me a jigsaw and I'll know what to do, but anything paranormal goes right over my head."

"You knew about shadow people."

"Just what I read on my phone. How did people deal with this stuff before the internet?" They started moving up the stairs, out of the basement. "What are we looking for?"

"Trudy thought something was going to happen in Perfect and I think it all stems from this place."

"So why is it happening at my house?"

"Maybe she found something and brought it home. Or something found her and followed her home."

"I don't like the sound of that, either way."

"You find anything in your house you've never seen before? It could be anything."

Danny slowly shook his head. "Nothing."

The two men stood in the living room of the Headington house. The room was empty. Relatively clean. Not even dust.

"This looks nothing like that movie." Danny sounded disappointed. Of course he had seen the movie, everyone in Perfect saw the movie, as it played at the Perfect Movie Theater for weeks.

"It's all in the terminology in Hollywood. That movie was *inspired* by a *true story*. In other words, it happened in Perfect and in this house, but the rest was up for grabs."

"That's good for us, right?"

"What do you mean?"

"The movie claimed demonic possession, but obviously it was just plain old homicide."

But Adam did not look convinced. He had seen too much to reject everything simply to have things make sense. But he had to admit that the Headington house did not have the *vibe*. "Can you take me back to my place? I have some equipment I think can help back at your house."

"So we're leaving here?"

"Yes."

"Good."

The drive to Echo Ridge was silent; they picked up Snowball because Danny did not want to leave her at the house. The dog sat in the backseat. Never moved, did not make a sound. Adam kept looking back at the dog during the drive.

"Your dog is simply too good!"

"I got lucky."

"And then some!"

At Adam's place, Danny parked in the street in front of the writer's house.

"I'll grab my equipment and drive back to Perfect in my car."

"Are you sure?"

"Go on ahead, I'll be no more than fifteen minutes behind you."

Danny waved and drove off, not realizing that he would not see Adam Burke again, but Adam's story was only beginning as he entered his house, and that was another story altogether.

Snowball started to growl the moment Danny drove back into Perfect.

"What's wrong?" Danny felt a chill run down his spine and he had to stop the car, parking in the Perfect High School parking lot for a moment. The dog jumped into the front seat and looked at Danny, as if trying to tell him something silently.

"We better get home or Mr. Burke might get there before us." Danny drove out of the parking lot to his house, parking and scooping Snowball up into his arms. Getting out of the car, Danny was shocked to find Teddy Jones sitting on the front porch, chin resting on his hands, a glum look on his face. "What are you doing here, Teddy?" Danny looked around, wondering why Teddy's parents had let him out at this time of night. It was only at that moment that Danny actually realized that night had indeed fallen. *How long had they been at the Headington house?*

"I'm sorry, Mr. Curry!" Teddy sounded like he was on the verge of crying.

"Sorry for what, Teddy?" Danny stood in front of Teddy, holding Snowball, the puppy growling softly, almost like a cat purring.

Teddy started shaking his head back and forth violently. "I knew it was bad, I shouldn't have done it!"

"Teddy... Teddy... calm down!" He had never seen Teddy so agitated before.

"I knew it was bad!"

"What, Teddy?"

"I'm the one who dug the hole by your house!" Teddy wailed and then burst into tears, burying his face in both hands.

"Why?"

"To put it under your house."

"What did you put under my house?"

"The book."

Danny was now completely confused. "What book, Teddy? Danny tried to sound calm, not wanting to get Teddy even more riled up.

"The book Mrs. Danny brought from the *bad house!*"

Danny tried to let everything Teddy said sink in, but he was having a hard time digesting it all. "How did you know she got the book from the bad house?"

"Because I was with her when she found it!"

Teddy went with Trudy to the Headington house? This revelation was almost like a punch in the gut to Danny.

"Why were you with her? You know no one is supposed to go in that house, Teddy."

Teddy Jones had been in love with Mrs. Danny. Whenever possible, he asked if he could do any chores for her. Teddy would do things like add water to Mrs. Danny's waterfall during the summer or take the garbage can out to the curb on Wednesdays. He followed her when she went out. More to protect her than anything else. Teddy never wanted anything bad to ever happen to Mrs. Danny, he loved her that much.

Teddy knew about the *bad house.* It was where the monsters lived. So when he saw Mrs. Danny crawl in through a window, Teddy knew that he had to follow, because he did not want the monsters to get her.

"Teddy, what are you doing here?" Mrs. Danny had said to him when he tried to follow, but got stuck in the small window.

"You shouldn't be here, Mrs. Danny! This place is bad!"

"I know, Teddy. That's why I'm here."

That confused Teddy. When Mrs. Danny helped pull him through the window, Teddy refused to leave, told Mrs. Danny that he would stay with her as long as she was in that house. She smiled that Mrs. Danny smile that always melted Teddy's heart and told him to stay close to her as they moved through the house. Teddy did not know why they were there, but it scared him. Badly.

"That house *felt wrong,* Mr. Danny!"

"What happened, Teddy?"

Teddy held onto Mrs. Danny's hand the entire time. He was filled with mixed emotions, even though he did not really understand why. Teddy almost swooned holding Mrs. Danny's hand, but he could also feel a rising terror the longer they stayed in the *bad house.* He wanted to say something, but kept silent and just followed Mrs. Danny as she moved from room to room in the house. Was she looking for something? Then Mrs. Danny told Teddy to stay where he was, that she was going up into the attic and did not want him to follow. Teddy did as he was told, but was terrified. The house seemed to be *alive,* although Teddy could not really form the words to properly explain that feeling he felt as he stood alone in the Headington house.

"When Mrs. Danny came back, she looked *awful!"*

"What do you mean, Teddy?"

Teddy knew what it was like to be scared, he had been scared most of his conscious life, but this was different. Mrs. Danny looked *scared to death.* Teddy had heard his mommy use those words before and they just seemed to be *right* at that moment. For the first time, Mrs. Danny looked *ugly* to

Teddy, because she was so scared. She grabbed Teddy by the hand and pulled him along, going out the front door, not even bothering to close it behind them, they were moving so fast. In Mrs. Danny's left hand was a book.

"What kind of book, Teddy?"

"An *ugly* book, Mr. Danny!"

Danny felt a growing terror. "Why did you bury it under the house, Teddy?"

"*BECAUSE IT TOLD ME TO!*"

Danny flinched. He tried to maintain a calm facade, but inside he was twisted with an erupting panic that threatened to detonate into a million screams. "When did you bury it, Teddy?"

"Just before you got Snowball."

Danny nodded. "Can you tell me exactly where you put it, Teddy?"

"Why?"

"Because I have to go get it."

"Oh, no! No, Mr. Danny! It's a *bad book!*"

"That's why I have to go get it, Teddy. Now, please, tell me."

Teddy told him.

Danny put Teddy and Snowball in his car and entered the house. He could hear the dog barking, as if in protest, as he closed the door behind him. Danny swiped at the switch. No lights. *We're going to play it that way, huh?* But simple parlor tricks were not going to stop Danny. He pulled out the nails he sealed the access panel with and dropped into the hole without hesitation. *It ends tonight, one way or the other!* Danny almost hesitated, the stench was so overpowering. *More tricks.* He knew that stink was not from a dead rat in a trap. He started crawling. In the back of his mind, Danny was surprised that Adam Burke had not shown up yet, but quickly pushed that aside as he saw that he was once again enveloped in a dense fog. *Is that all you got?* Danny kept moving. He then heard heavy footsteps over his head. "I don't believe in you!" Danny shouted.

But we believe in you, Daniel!

That did make Danny stop. The voice had been in his head.

"Why did you kill my wife?" There was no fear in Danny's voice, just righteous anger. "You're not going to answer me? Danny started crawling again.

Do you want to see her again, Daniel? We can make that happen.

Danny reached the spot Teddy said where he buried the book and Danny started to dig with his bare hands. He grimaced. It felt like he was digging through a squirming mass of maggots that crawled all over his hands, up his arms, toward his face. Then he felt it, the book, and pulled it free from the earth. Danny started to back out.

She wants to see you, Daniel!

Danny ignored the voice. He knew that he had to back up about ten feet before he could turn around. But then he ran into something. Solid. But... *living.* Slowly, Danny reached behind him with his free hand. It felt like a wall of sheer muscle. Danny gritted his teeth and resumed his moving backward, right through whatever was blocking him. *Just illusions.* Danny turned around and quickly crawled to the opening and climbed out. He paused and looked at the book in his hand. Danny made a face of revulsion. The book was indeed *ugly,* just like Teddy had said. Danny wanted to open it, see what was inside, but forced himself not to, moving to the back door and going out into the back yard.

It knows what I'm going to do.

Danny expected one last assault, but none came as he moved to the fire pit just to the left of Trudy's waterfall. He tossed the book into the circle of stacked stones. A squirt of lighter fluid from his work shed, a match struck to life, and the book was ablaze. No incredible display, no hideous figure rising in the smoke and flames, just a burning book. It was quite anti-climatic, to say the least.

"Is it gone?"

Danny turned to see Teddy standing a few feet away, Snowball in his arms. Danny nodded.

"I think so."

"But it really isn't gone, you know."

Danny frowned. Teddy sounded *normal,* and that scared Danny. "What do you mean?"

"This is only the beginning here in Perfect." Teddy then set the dog down and walked off.

Snowball ran up to Danny, who bent over and picked up the puppy. Danny stood there in the back yard for a long time, and then went into the house. The lights came on when Danny hit the switch. He went upstairs and changed, turning on the TV and placing Snowball on the bed. The dog did her usual spinning around several times and then curled up and went to sleep. Danny smiled. He stretched out on the bed and watched TV. His eyes grew heavy and closed.

That night, Trudy came to Danny in his dreams.

THE END

Printed in Great Britain
by Amazon